18.60

Melvin's Cold Feet

**For a free color catalog describing Gareth Stevens' list
of high-quality children's books, call 1-800-341-3569
(USA) or 1-800-461-9120 (Canada).**

Library of Congress Cataloging-in-Publication Data

Crust, Linda.
    Melvin's cold feet / written by Linda Crust ; illustrated
by John Brindle. — U.S. ed.
        p. cm.
    Summary: A spider finds a way to help a mouse with
cold feet.
    ISBN 0-8368-0356-6
    [1. Mice—Fiction. 2. Spiders—Fiction.] I. Brindle, John,
ill. II. Title.
PZ7.C8897Me   1991
[E]—dc20   90-47201

North American edition first published in 1991 by
Gareth Stevens Children's Books
1555 North RiverCenter Drive, Suite 201
Milwaukee, Wisconsin 53212, USA

U.S. edition copyright © 1991. First published in Great Britain in 1989 by Macdonald
Children's Books, Simon & Schuster International Group, with an original text copyright
© 1989 by Linda Crust. Illustrations copyright © 1989 by John Brindle.

Printed in the United States of America

1 2 3 4 5 6 7 8 9 95 94 93 92 91

MELVIN'S COLD FEET

LINDA CRUST & JOHN BRINDLE

Gareth Stevens Children's Books
MILWAUKEE

When Melvin
Mouse and his
nine brothers and
sisters were born,
they were pink and had no hair. They
looked just like tiny piglets. When they
curled up together near their mother,
it was almost impossible to tell which
mouse was which.

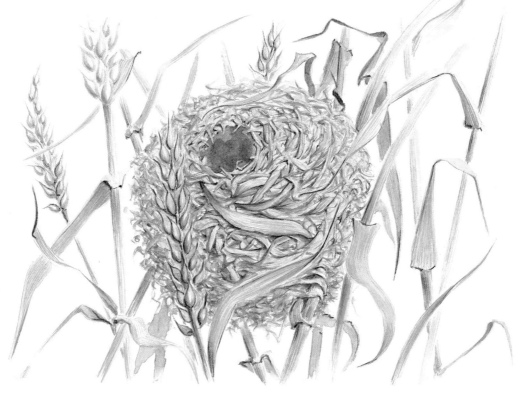

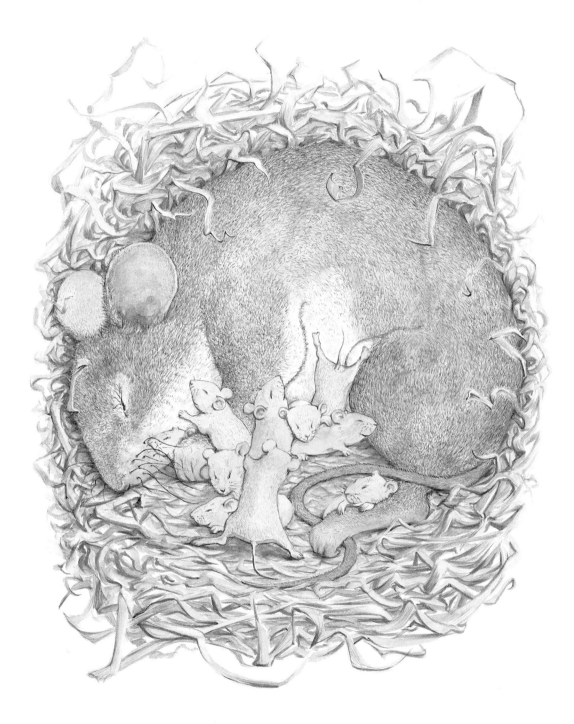

But all the baby mice knew which
one was which. They especially
knew which one was Melvin. Melvin
had such cold feet.

"Get off, Melvin," they would squeak.
"We don't like your cold feet."

Even Mother Mouse sometimes said, "Melvin, I can feel your cold feet on my tummy."

But she was his mother, and she
loved him. So she let him warm his
toes in her soft fur.

Soon Melvin grew up, and it was time for him to leave the nest. His father told him, "Make sure you find somewhere nice and warm to live, Melvin. Otherwise, those cold feet will keep you awake all night."

15

So Melvin set out to find a warm
place to make his first nest.

Melvin scuttled off to a pretty little house nearby. He was sure his feet would stay nice and warm there. The door was open, so he dashed inside. There he found a basket full of wool.

"This is perfect for a mouse with cold feet," he thought as he curled up in the warm wool. He slept soundly that night. He even had a nibble of green wool for supper and a nibble of red wool for breakfast.

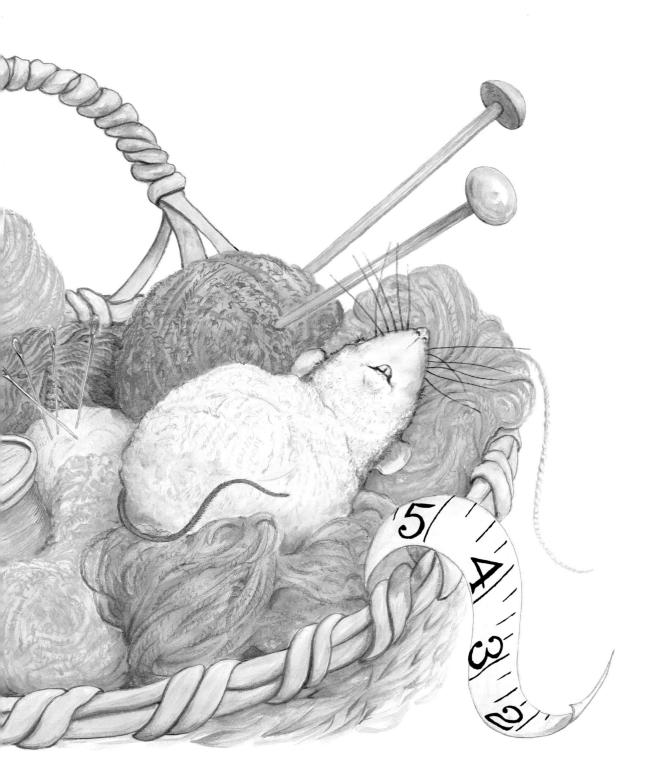

The next day, the woman who lived
in the house had some socks to mend.
She looked into her mending basket
and saw Melvin. She
screamed and
screamed.

Poor Melvin awoke with a start. He jumped from the basket and ran from the house as fast as he could.

Melvin met his friend the spider and told him all about it.

"If I didn't have such cold feet," he said, "I could live in a field or a barn. What can I do?"

The spider was kind.
  "I'll spin you some socks,"
he said. "They will keep your
feet warm."

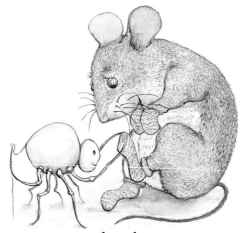

The spider spun
two fine pairs of
socks for Melvin.
They fit him perfectly.
With his new socks,
Melvin was able to
settle down in a very airy corner of the
garden shed.

And his feet were never cold again.